# DOWN THE PATH OF LIFE

**Other titles by the Author**
**Nonfiction:**
Destination: My Journey Across the Globe
**Fiction:**
Down the Path of Life, Season's Fall
Down the Path of Life, Season's Frost
Down the Path of Life, Season's Heat
The Teenage Militia

# DOWN THE PATH OF LIFE

## OF LIFE

### SEASON'S SPRING

# J. A. IRVIN

ISBN: 9798450810805



First published on 06/27/2015 by CreatSpace.com
Cover art copyright © 2021 by Clayton Foy Udd

Printed in United States of America.

All scripture quotations marked KJV are from the Holy Bible, King James Version (Authorized Version). First published in 1611.
This is a work of fiction. Names, characters, places, and incidents either are the product of the author's imagination or are used fictitiously, and any resemblance to any actual persons, living or dead, events, or locales is entirely coincidental.
Print information available on the last page.

I dedicate this book to my wife, a very dear person,
One who encourages and challenges me,
And who stands by me through hard and easy times.
She will always be close to my heart.

# PROLOGUE

*Season's Spring* continues the journey *Down The Path Of Life*. With changing seasons come changing paths and new opportunities. Sometimes the changing path's beginnings are mysterious and frightening, yet lead to excitement and joyful prospects; however, the benefits cannot be gleaned without the courage to change course. Through a collection of over twenty-five poems, the author shows his passion, interests, and thoughts. Poems such as "Contemplation of Life and a Bed of Roses" and "That of This Forest World" speak of important life lessons he learned from nature, and other poems such as "Oh Daddy, Can't You Remember" and "Daddy, Me and You" pay tribute to fatherhood.

Nine short stories comprise the second portion of this volume. Filled with adventure, horror, romance, and action, these stories are sure to entertain. "William and Boonesborough, Part 5" and "William and Boonesborough, Part 6" continue the saga of William and his growing family. Part 5 tells of William's childhood memories as he shares the story of how he and Jenny endured the orphan home, and all the while growing in love with each other. William and his sons go on a hunting expedition in Part 6, only to find that someone else has stirred up a momma bear and is causing immediate danger to everyone in the area.

Elbridge Lawrence is being haunted on his hike in the forest, and is sure it is the living dead. The "Fear of the Unseen" could cost Elbridge his life as his fear takes him off the path and over a ravine.

As the smoke from cannons and muskets still lingers across the battlefield, but not one able body remains, those still with breath in their lungs must look out for themselves, or for their fellow man. Soldiers find that the colors of the uniform do not matter in the battle for life in "As You Would Them To You."

"The Feeling Within" narrates the mental struggle that a young Israeli girl has as she begins to fall in love with a British officer. Her love for this young man clashes with the resentment that she has for the large British presence in her homeland. She knows her heart wants what it wants, but realizes her culture must be preserved.

The Jewish people have always found hardship and heartache wherever they settled, and many of their settlements have been pushed away. "The Program" shows a little of this struggle as one population reacts to the Jewish differences.

From the beginning of time, people have wondered what is beyond the horizon. In "On A Long Journey," Clay and Katherine embraced the adventures of searching for a new life. The West is rough, but news that family is on their way for a visit might bring some joy.

Sailing farther back in time, a Spanish conquistador is commissioned to journey to the New World in search of a legendary relic. "The Mythical or Genuine Relic" is rumored to bestow world renowned fame and power to any in possession of it, but is the deadly trek that lay ahead of them worth the risk?

John Ashworth realizes it is blood that will free the Colonies from the tyranny of Great Britain, and he is willing to pay that price for his family. However, "A Price Paid At Concord" is almost too much of a burden for him to bear.

# Contents

## SHORT STORIES

# Selected Poems

# On My Graduation

This is my beginning, with happiness and joy,
Now goes my youth, no longer am I just a boy.
It is now my time to take on me,
This other dissimilar responsibility

I am pleased to look back on my years and deem,
They were spent with some small ray or beam.
And will help brighten my days to come,
My future days with its dark day some.

And on this stage of life as I walk along,
I think of the people who in my life have belong.
The people who have helped in my maturing,
And now I thank God for their existing.

# Tears of this Child Girl

*I watched tears glisten this child's cheeks,*
*And could not help but think how God did send,*
*He sent this girl for a reason,*
*She was a heartfelt descend.*

*Those tears of her eyes were something special,*
*Not of within, out of pity or self-will,*
*But for another,*
*For another she feels.*

*The teardrops fall with a meaning,*
*Her heart is hurt for that person in pain,*
*For that other she is crying,*
*The other feelings are hers the same.*

*That little girl is such a special child,*
*How selfless her will as she felt for that other,*
*Cannot we have feelings as well,*
*Cannot we think of another?*

# Thank You For Your Pictures

*Thank you, Jesus, for your beautiful creation,*
*Thank you, Jesus, for each picture you show me,*
*Each has a special meaning of what you have done,*
*Of how you love and care for me.*

*Each picture has its own paints and strokes,*
*Each picture a different brush and design,*
*Unique in their way, but all with that same meaning,*
*Wonder filled of his love divine.*

*You have proven your love over and over.*
*A picture just now fades from my view,*
*Please always keep me in your steps to follow,*
*Never leave me, always keep me near you.*

# That Flag that Flies for You and Me

Can you remember that very day?
And where you were
When the terror came,
From those crashing planes.
Did you think the end was near that day?
As you watched that scene,
That took those lives away.

Now I loudly shout, stand up!
And hold that flag so near!
That flag that flew that day,
Still flies today so dear!

At that time our lives were turned upside down,
As we watched those towers fall,
But the harm wasn't over,
Because of the other that fell as well.
At that time when our lives were turned around,
Was there something we lost?
Did our faith fall to the ground?

No! So let us proudly stand up and shout,
Hail that flag that flies so free!
That flag that fell that day,
Still flies for you and me!

# Contemplation of Life and A Bed of Roses

*Life, a bed of roses—can it be?*
*Let us perhaps think of this, shall we?*
*To ponder on such a phrase as this,*
*Is only true for someone now to do,*
*Only right for someone now to write.*
*There are the petals, comfortable and velvety,*
*Soft to lie in—dare I say, the envy of piety.*
*Life is pleasure to do and rest in leisure of day,*
*To smile and laugh as going about life's way.*

*There are the sentiments of color,*
*Some may know all, the orange telling desire,*
*Red—as known to most, shows ones love,*
*White is unity and pure as the heavens above,*
*And there is yellow, for care is it to show.*

*Though we must continue on 'to lounge in roses'.*
*There are not just petals as one supposes,*
*But the stems and thorns are there,*
*The stabs of life and pricking pains,*
*The hurts and the losses with life's gains.*

*So we have the petals—the stem—the thorn,*
*And we have to live and take all that's born.*
*We have to face and accept every hard way,*

*Though we should only do what is only true,*
*As we face what we have to face.*
*But enjoy the moments of pleasure and ease,*
*Enjoy the happiness, enjoy what you please,*
*And remember from where it all comes,*
*That may decide what all becomes.*

# A Star, A Cross, And A Crown

As I passed, I glanced and there they were,
A star, a cross, and a crown,
Three things that tell the reason why I am still around.
They have meant so much to the faith I have today,
Meant so much and gave me strength to live day by day.

The star that shone bright to those kings from the East,
The star that helped them find the King among the least.
That what showed the way to those searching three,
That what proclaimed that King to be.

And the cross where that King willingly went,
That rugged tree where hung the Saviour that was sent.
The tree at Golgotha where His body was taken from,
That tree, empty, where His body never stayed on.

And the crown, His glory that came when He arose.
It that proves He conquered our spiritual foes.
A crown that one day I hope to be able to receive,
A crown to lay before the One in whom I believe.

I passed these objects very brightly displayed,
And they mean so much when thoughtfully weighed.

# A Cross

*I pass a cross as I drive down the highway,*
*Who might that person have been?*
*A stranger to me, and unknown to others,*
*But perhaps a dad, mom, daughter, or son.*

*The grave was marked only by a small, white cross,*
*What might have this person had?*
*No fame, no wealth, no house or kin,*
*No comforts, 'tis indeed a saddened sin.*

*The cross was weathered, no flowers to shine,*
*Was this person loved in this world left behind?*
*Did he have someone to care for all his needs?*
*Someone to listen to all his heeds?*

# At That Place

Well, this place was fine and grand, and I enjoyed my stay here
so good,
But now it's my turn to up and move, it's just something I
should.
Now the house wasn't large or giant to me,
There weren't any pillars or porches to see,
No oak doors, or marble floors, or chandeliers there be.
There was no parlor, or ball dance room,
No winding case stairs, or grand hearth with flume.
There was no study, with its thousands of books,
No elegant paintings, hung only for looks.
There was no room with its large posted bed,
No dining with its cherry table, or wonderful spread,
No servants to call, when laziness I feel,
No bedroom pamper, or in bed meal.
No, there weren't these things, just a little, old place,
Just one small house, with three bedroom space,
Just a bit of a porch and a single, simple door,
Just a plain entry and a bit of linoleum floor,
Only a small room to dine, with a four seating table,
Only a squeaking bed, but where rest was very able.
There is only this house, with its plain walls, but strong,
Only a house, but it could last for long.

*Now the land, there wasn't much as my dreams could be,*
*No acres of land, to run and make me feel mighty and free,*
*No orchards so grand, no apples, pears, or cherry tree.*
*There weren't any fields, in which to send men,*
*There weren't any places, or horses to pen,*
*No, not any pride to breed, or national races to run,*
*No, not that enjoyment, or feeling as if the world is won.*
*No, there weren't these things, but there was more,*
*On this grand, ole' land there were beauties galore.*
*At this happy, small place there was a lake that shines,*
*There were fish to catch and frogs and ducks that whine.*
*There were birds in the trees and cool evening breeze,*
*There was quietness and something extra more to please.*
*At that place there was a view with little compare,*
*To look off that mountain and see the sun waning there.*
*It was something wonderful to watch the sun go down,*
*Something serene when the earth was sound.*
*Yes, indeed, I very much enjoyed my stay up there,*
*And I will miss the nature and some people who cared.*

# That of This Forest World

If I were to walk among the shade of the trees,
And allow the darkness to cover my soul.
Thinking only for now, and I'll find my way out,
But would that darkness engulf and control?

All the charms of the nature of this forest,
Oh, I think and ponder on them now.
I'll find my pleasure and make my way out,
Oh, the beauties there, and to leave the foul.

The foul of this land I would leave behind,
Cardinals and red breasts with their harsh song.
Songs so disturbing and hurtful to my sound,
The sounds of this nature, so tiring and long.

And to listen to the forest for the sounds so clear,
Voices of a hawk, preying on its kill.
The cry of the kill as it's grasped in the claws,
And as it then loses its life and will.

Happiness I would feel if I may then leave,
The horrid sight of this tamed, flower plot,
Unsightly are its colors and pain filled petals,
The bitter filled scent of such this terrible lot.

*I am thinking of now, and sure I'll find*
*That soft and lovely plant, poison vine.*
*That poison ivy so pleasing to the touch,*
*A feel of wonder, and the figure more fine.*

*Oh the fruit of this unsightly orchard,*
*Oh the acrid taste of any fruit I bite in.*
*I feel to step on and bruise all this bitter fruit,*
*Just give me a part, what could be sin?*

*Just give me a moment to then go and taste,*
*And savor the flavor of that juicy poison thing.*
*That poisonous mushroom so delicious to my taste,*
*To all of this forest world let me slightly cling.*

# Little Ray of Sunshine

*I am thinking now of a little ray of sunshine,*
*Who brightened my path and lightened my way,*
*In my uncertain path and darker day,*
*A little glowing beam and small shining ray.*

*Not sure where I'd be or what I'd done,*
*Stumbling along without that glow from the Son,*
*That small shining glow that was begun,*
*When He knew I truly needed that One.*

*Now I am praying to the dear, heavenly Being,*
*Give me the reflection for my future seeing,*
*Because my future days are now shadowing,*
***And that shining reflection I shall be needing.***

# My Responsibility

*It's my responsibility to pay the rent,*
*Mine to see money is wisely spent.*
*It's my responsibility to pay bills on time,*
*Mine to pay all to the very last dime.*

*It's my responsibility to put food on the table,*
*Mine to buy a pop when even possible.*
*It's my responsibility to clean my clothes,*
*Mine to make sure a spot never shows.*

*It's my responsibility to get to my job on time,*
*Mine to make sure I clock out on time.*
*It's my responsibility to put property away,*
*Mine to get things ready for the following day.*

# Oh Daddy,
# Can't You Remember

Oh Daddy, can't you remember, that day you were told,
How you waited forever, can't waiting to hold.
Then oh how the months flew by, and finally she came,
Can't you remember when you held her nothing was the same.
You looked into her eyes, love and joy filled your heart,
She had a love of her own, in you, she had a part.

Oh Daddy, can't you remember that day you brought her home,
When you laid her in her crib and her little eyes shone.
Can't you remember you watching as she grew,
From the crib to a bed, my how those years then flew.
Can't you remember holding her hand as she walked beside
you,
Do you remember her asking, when everything to her was new.

Oh Daddy, can't you remember putting that growing girl to
sleep,
Kissing good night and leaving her to God's care and keep.
Can't you remember when she would say, 'I love you',
How those words echoed in your heart, her love to you was
true.
Then as that darling girl grew, you knew that time would soon
arrive,

16

*How you wanted the time to slow, how you wished those times revive.*
*And oh Daddy, can't you remember that day she saw him,*
*All her words to you were of him, did her love for you grow dim?*
*Then their times together grew, and she began to spend less with you,*
*No longer sharing her heart, no longer, with you.*
*And now Daddy, this day of difference has finally came,*
*How you miss all the memories, you wish all were the same.*

# A Blessing For Marriage

Dear kind and gently, sir and lady,
As you join in holy matrimony,
May the Almighty, who reins from above,
Peer below and strengthen your enduring love.

May He bless you two especially,
As you now bond divinely.
May He keep your love continuing,
And maintain your trust everlasting.

As this time comes and you stand there,
May you not only gaze on the beauty, but dare
To gaze upon the soul that is with each within,
And wish to know the good as this new life you begin.

For in this new life, it is only the good
That in dark days, keeps the sun shining, as should.
And in the days when you are low and down,
It is the good that will pick all off the ground.

May God bless you as you look on the good of life,
And as you join and battle all the toil and strife,
And may you follow in life, where He shows,
Because everywhere, He is and everything, He knows.

# God's Existence

Do not you enjoy when God shows His existence?
Does not it make you feel, inside, less resistance?
When even small things occur,
God's power does assure.

In every little something there is a mighty power.
In every blade of grass and in the beauty of a flower,
In every song of a bird,
And every voice that's heard.

When God spoke creation into form,
The moon to light and the sun to warm.
When He created the man
In the likeness of His form.

In all His creation there is some small hint
That at times will show, because he meant.
The greatness of His power,
Even in each flower.

# My Relief

Where is my relief?<br>
There's none is my belief.<br>
Something to ease my great headache.<br>
But all is just a fake.

I tried the caffeine drinks.<br>
They only took me to many brinks.<br>
I tried repeated naps.<br>
They only caused lip chaps.

Please heal this bad headache.<br>
It causes the room to shake.<br>
Any noise is gruesome to hear.<br>
My eardrums may pop I fear.

So I'll try holy wedlock.<br>
Oh wow, I receive great shock!<br>
This great headache has ceased.<br>
I hope for sixty years at least.

# Daddy, Me and You

Daddy worked long hours of the day.
Many times he would be called away.
His call took him from the ones he loved,
But every return was more beloved.

Daddy traveled many times a week.
He served God and encouraged the weak,
But every time he was away,
He missed the ones who loved him anyway.

Daddy preached in many far states,
Speaking how God can change all fates.
And every time a sinner repented,
The angels in heaven all celebrated.

When Daddy returned, his family came first,
Their love and affection, their attention thirst.
He took his family to places of fun.
He took each child, not one to shun.

And Daddy that day chose his child,
His youngest girl, not meek or wild.
They spent together, making happy memories,
Their time together, she gave his hand a squeeze.

*Daddy looked in his child's eyes and grinned.*
*She looked to him with a joy-filled blend,*
*She opened her mouth and spoke love so true,*
*"Daddy, I like it when it's just me and you."*

# Look What God Gave Me

There lived a family unknown to fame,
But they lived along and had some to claim.
No wealth, or riches, or honors renown,
But they had a family and a place to call their own.

This family was young, not having many years.
Not aged in all knowledge, and with some fears.
Yet they were steady and loved each other.
The love was strong and held them close together.

They had no frivolous items, yet each a special toy.
Dolls, had the girls, and perhaps cars, had the boy.
They enjoyed their toys with hours of fun,
Each liked what they had, yet all had a favorite one.

One young girl played house in every free moment.
Her dolls were special, yet with two, most enjoyment.
She loved those two and never could think to part.
To those very little two she gave her heart.

Yet a special day came, the two were asked for,
To help adorn a wedding cake, giving spirit more.
She teared, yet with a promise for their return,
Gave for joy, yet what was she then to learn.

The two united, after then saw with glee,
And asked for the doll man and lady their's to be,
That little girl then wished to cry,
Yet smiled and gave without asking why.

The parents were sorry, yet promised the child,
They bought her more wishing to make sorrow mild.
Her smile returned when she saw with glee,
And said "Daddy, look what God gave me."

# The World Is Dead

The world is dead,
Snow hops to the ground.
The world is dead,
Last leaves fall all around.

The world is dead,
Five thousand students around.
The world is dead,
All eyes face the ground.

The world is dead,
No voices can be heard.
The world is dead,
No voices, no spoken word.

The world is dead,
Though humans all beside.
The world is dead,
All noises now reside.

# Who Are You

You grab attention from the beginning sound.
I am captivated by the power you hold.
The sound of notes flying all around,
You votives sent so high and held so bold.


My breath is paused, happy at the gladness,
Your sound fills laughter within my heart.
How could you do this to me?
The gladness you make me feel so much a part.


Oh, then the drastic thing happens,
The story turns and the octaves lower.
The whispers come and the sound's sad,
I feel the tears, the story seems slower.


How could they do this and hurt you?
You were the perfect one, and to him the only.
You did only the good in your heart,
Oh, the heartbreak, oh, the great lonely.


But then you triumph and sound grows,
You laugh a little and continue on.
The octaves are at their medium pitch.
I smile, knowing you will live on.

*The time comes to end your story.*
*You blast and then begin your fade.*
*This was all great pleasant to listen to.*
*Who are you, the story you made? You are Music!*

# My Promise

*I'll be with you to the end.*
*I'll be with you my dear friend.*
*Though the clouds of darkness come,*
*And the rain and gusts of wind,*
*I'll be with you to the end.*
*I'll be with you my loved friend.*
*Though the loud stormy rage,*
*And the dry gusty sage,*
*I'll be with you my loved friend.*
*I'll be with you through thick and thin.*
*When all other friendships end,*
*When you don't know where to turn,*
*I'll be with you in thick and thin.*

# Going Away

*"Mommy, where are you going?"*
*A young girl questioned.*
*Mommy's hat was on and all was showing*
*That she was leaving, yet*
*Skies were dark and night was coming.*

*Mommy leaned down to kiss a cheek,*
*And paused briefly before answering.*
*Mommy has to leave for a time,*
*Mommy is going away for a time unknowing,*
*Mommy has to go away.*

*"Mommy, why are you going?"*
*The young girl questioned.*
*Mommy sat near and stared unknowing,*
*This mommy once knew all, yet*
*A fog had drifted and night was coming.*

*Mommy took a glance at her innocent child,*
*She did not want any hurting.*
*Mommy can't live this life right now,*
*She can't live life without understanding,*
*Mommy has to go away.*

"But mommy where are you going?"
She questioned with tear in eye.
Mommy paused, her heart was tearing,
This mommy knew not, yet
She knew her child would worry of her dwelling.

Mommy brushed hair off the child's face.
She answered with words needing least explaining.
Mommy will live in a place so good,
She will have comfort, so please no worrying,
Please, mommy must go away.

Mommy turned and walked to the door.
Tears burned as they ran down her cheek.
She may never see her child anymore.
But she had not strength to turn back.
The problems were big and she was weak.

The child stood and ran to mother.
"Mommy don't go," she begged and pleaded.
"I'll be better," she cried to the other.
Mommy stopped, briefly enough to turn,
"It isn't you; it's something else I needed."

Mommy turned and went out the door.
The daughter's heart was breaking.
For mommy's return, she was wishing, yet
Mommy had chosen her life.
And mommy was gone.

The young girl watched from the window,
As mommy's last form was disappearing.
No sleep for her that night, instead there was crying.
Many questions were made in her mind, yet
For all there was no understanding.

The next week a big bus came,
And on her door there were people knocking,
To a place of worship, her, they were inviting.
She followed and learned from their teaching,
Of the One who will never go away.

# Some Fun

Sliding down the slope,
Slithering on the sled,
Slicing on the slide,
Sledding, not so slow.

Our sleds flew down the slope,
So fast we slid along,
So fun we all did sled,
Then slow we arched up slope.

Faster we flew together,
Fun with you our friends,
Flying so fast and free,
Fantastic our fellowship.

# Tribute

This is to all those who are good to me.
Beginning first to thank my family,
Those who were there in my beginning.
And to them, who may be in my ending,
I want to thank the family of my blood,
Those who provided a bed and food;
Those who supported in happy or foul mood.
Gratitude goes out to those who completed,
To them who married, helped, and supported;
The ones, through love, the family train boarded.
My happiness goes also to friends held close,
Those few in number, their support I boast;
I thank them each for their lives they share,
In smiles they joy and sadness they care.
And thanks to all friends and family of mine,
But to the one I found whose here to shine,
Sparkling like stars and clearing my night;
Clearing the fog and brightening the light,
Thank you my helper in my dark life,
Reminding me my way and loving me in strife.

# Something Mysterious

*You can travel the world and still miss*
*Something so important to human life.*
*You can travel, but find no bliss,*
*You can climb the highest mountain,*
*Or sail the hardest seas.*

*You can fly into space,*
*You can search the moon or stars above.*
*You will not find it in that place.*
*This something that fires as the sun,*
*Nearing the earth its heats and burns.*

*And it is something as unexpected,*
*Something we know is present, but cannot grasp,*
*The all of it is not completely discovered.*
*And if this is unclear and my subject unknown,*
*What is more mysterious than love?*

# What Everyone Knows

*Life changes, there's something everyone knows.*
*You grow, you walk, you run, and leap.*
*You sit around the table talking to the ones you know.*
*And suddenly the table is smaller, the changes don't creep.*
*One day you're working or playing with one family so dear,*
*Then next you are working for another family that's there.*
*One day you're caring in the country and a house,*
*Then next you're in the city, helping wife choose a blouse.*
*I'm not saying the new life is wrong,*
*Nor do I sit and wonder where I belong.*
*I'm just saying there's a change in life to watch the cars go by,*
*To hear ground motors, and to think I used to fly,*
*To live in a one room with neighbors three feet outside,*
*To live on your phone with your friend close beside.*
*I have a happy life now and wouldn't change it at all,*
*But it sure is different always running to the mall.*

# Answered That Call

You have answered that call,
That call of the King.
Each time a soul is reached,
The angels do sing.

You have answered that call,
And have earnestly gone,
To a land far away,
A land far beyond.

You have answered that call,
And left the comforts and ease,
But it isn't all for not,
Because your Saviour, ye do please.

# Outside My Window

*Calming drops outside my window,*
*Ease my stress, they now do flow.*
*The drops place peace in now my soul,*
*Those pleasant drops outside my window.*

*Now they are here to wash the sin,*
*Reminding Christians we will win.*
*Rain of past that wiped those men*
*From this earth and all their sin.*

*That rain came down and purged the earth,*
*Keeping alive only who God deemed worth.*
*Claiming those with much Christian dearth,*
*The rain that poured, wiped this sinful earth.*

*But now this rain outside my window,*
*No earth destroyed with its passing flow,*
*Only pleasant drops, it soothes my soul.*
*Praise God for the rain outside my window.*

# A Stranger of the Present

A different man drives down life's roads,
Different than all others around.
Speaking the same, but different in time,
Different on earth of others found.

There's a stranger walking the path of life,
A stranger among a present day.
Talking the same, but a stranger of time,
A stranger of all, walking his own way.

There's an alien that lives upon this land,
Alien to the present, should time rewind?
How did this man come to live
In this now, and not in the times behind?

# WILLIAM AND BOONESBOROUGH
# PART 5

*P*A, tell us a story."

"Yes father, please! Please!" the two young twins chorused in reply to the request of Samuel Boone Gerret.

William smiled as he sat little Beth on his knee.

"All right. Which story would you want to hear tonight?"

"The one of you and Ma at the bad orphan home!" Beth recommended excitingly.

He turned to glance at his beautiful wife who was finishing up cleaning the dishes off in the adjoining kitchen.

She returned his smile with a small shrug and a grin, and turned back to the dish in her hand.

William turned back to their three children. "Okay, although I will remind you all that this is the third time in the past two weeks that you have made that request."

"We don't care," they said in accordance.

Beth stated, "We wanna hear about that mean old man who was very bad to you and Mom, how you survived for a long time, and then how you fell in love and took her away."

"Yes, we want to hear about that," Seth agreed with just as much excitement as his sister.

"Well," William began, "I guess one more time for the week will not hurt anything. As long as you all promise to go off to bed right after I finish."

"We promise!" the three said in unison.

William took one look at his three children: Samuel, the oldest by a year; Seth, the slightly eldest twin; and Beth. Seth was leaned up against his oldest brother for comfort, and Beth leaned against her father, waiting for him to begin his story.

"My mother and father passed away with the chicken pox back when I was no older than you twins."

"So you were five!" Seth interrupted.

"Yes, that's right. Now, let me tell the story." William looked down at him with a smile.

"I was five years old when my parents died. Even though I did not fully understand just why they left me, I knew life changed so much for me that year. I did not have any other family members that I was told of, so the community took me to the orphan home."

"Which was a bad one!" Seth once again interjected.

"Well, it was not at the time that I was taken there, but let me continue without interrupting me from now on," William said lovingly.

"Sorry."

"Very well. Now, at the time that I was taken to the orphanage, a sweet elderly couple was the care providers. They were both very good to us and taught us many important life qualities. They taught us how to work, but did it in such a way that made us enjoy it, and we were able to reap the benefits of our labor.

"It was one tragic day when the sweet elderly man had a heart attack and passed into eternity. The widow then could not continue to help us alone, and she hired a younger man who eventually talked her into selling him the place and moving away from there.

"Once he was finally able to convince her to move away, the whole way of order changed. He became very mean to us and began to have us try different forms of work in order to try to make him rich. When he found out nothing we tried would last, he rented us out as hired labor. Usually the people who rented us were not too concerned about our well-being.

"Life became terrible with him as the 'master' of the home. Not only were we rented out as hired labor, we did things around the land for him, plus kept the house in an orderly disorder as it was.

"He would never allow us to attend church, as was the regular with the past caregivers. Years passed by, and the longer I served my 'master,' the more I began to hate him.

"Then one day, a pretty little girl showed up at that orphan home. I hated seeing her there, and yet at the same time I thought God had sent me an angel. I instantly began feelings for her. I slowly acquired to get to know her, and eventually we became good friends. With her being there, the work became even harder in my mind because I knew she had to do the same as well.

"When the master rented her out, somehow every time I managed to convince him to rent me out to the same people, and the more we worked together, the more I grew to love her. From what I understand," he said, while glancing over to Jenny, who had joined the family by that time. "She began to grow in love with me."

She nodded her head in agreement.

"What happened then, Papa?" little Seth questioned, begging for his father to continue the story.

"Well, there wasn't much left. When I got older, we escaped, came here, and married."

"But Papa," Seth queried, "What about the mean master's threat of sending Mama away and you standing up against him?"

William chuckled. "You almost know this story better than I do."

"Please continue, Papa," Beth pleaded. "Be quiet, Seth," she scolded.

"Okay. Well one day the mean master had rented us out, and the renter wanted to 'adopt,' or rather, purchase, me from the home, and the master agreed. One of our friends had overheard the bargaining between the two men and knew it meant trouble. He passed the information on to your mother and I, and I quickly set about trying to conceive a plan to escape.

"I knew it would be dangerous, but I also knew that it would even be more dangerous not to do anything at all. I enlisted the help of planning for it from only a few of my most trusted friends, because I knew that several of the children would tell on us if it meant they would get some small treat, or in fear that they would be hurt if they didn't tell.

"The night finally came, and I slipped out of the home unnoticed. I had to leave your mother behind, because I had no idea of what was in the outside world, and I was not sure how we both would have survived.

"I ran away from the town and found a big city where I employed in odd jobs and such to keep myself alive and to save some. I met Daniel Boone when I was purchasing my first gun and followed him out here to Kentucky. He invited me to work with him for awhile, until a decided I needed to return for your mother.

"On my journey back I was very worried that she might not be there anymore. I also worried that the master might have hurt her because of my leaving. When I returned in the dead of night, I just happened to see your mother up in a window, and managed to help her escape.

"We managed to find our way all the way back here and were married, and are now living happily ever after with three beautiful children."

He looked around at his three young children, and found them to be mostly asleep.

"All right. You promised to go off to bed after the story," he said to all of them.

Tiredly, the boys rose up and made their way to their room. Beth, however, clung to his neck, so he picked her up, carried her to her room, and laid her gently on her bed. He kissed her goodnight and exited the room. He waited as his wife assisted their daughter to change clothing for the night, and then he walked with Jenny to their room.

It was their turn to ready for bed, and as they were doing so, Jenny spoke. "I enjoy listening to you tell stories to our children."

He paused with his present task and looked to her. "Thank you. I did not know I was such a great orator."

She grinned to his joke, yet stated, "Not just for your orator skills, but to keep our past fresh in our minds. I never want to forget where we came from. It helps me to appreciate where we are now."

He planted a soft kiss on her lips, and during their embrace, he agreed, "Indeed it does."

"Goodnight, my love."

"Goodnight, my dear."

# WILLIAM AND BOONESBOROUGH PART 6

*F*ATHER, do you think we will see some bears on our journey?" young Seth asked his father, William.

"Oh Seth there are no bears here," the older son, Samuel Boone Gerret, rebuked. "The Indian killed or scared them all off. Isn't that right, father?"

William searched for a moment and then grinned with satisfaction. "Actually, there may be a few left. Look down there." Saying that, he pointed to a fresh set of paw prints. "Now, if I am not mistaken, those belong to a large black bear, who is searching for a complete meal of two young boys who like to fight each other all the time." he teased, and finishing up with poking playfully at the oldest and ruffling the hair of the youngest.

They both laughed and admired the set of paw prints.

"And it was not the Indians who killed off all the bear. It was the white men," William continued to teach. "You see, the Indians learned to live along with the wildlife of the forest, but the well-educated white people, like us, tend to scare easily or just kill for the sport of killing."

The two young lads looked puzzled at William's lesson, but the younger one voiced his concerns. "Then why are we killing animals?"

William smiled at his son's acknowledgement. "We only kill what we can and need to eat, no more. And we are careful not to waste."

This seemed to satisfy the two so they continued in their hunt.

Their search was slow in finding the perfect deer to feed the number in their family. They found some small and some large, but it was not until the evening when William finally decided the one before them was right, and he allowed Seth to take the shot.

Seth took aim, but was slightly nervous as he pulled the trigger, so he only grazed the deer.

Just as soon as William saw the deer bolt away, he started out after it, with his two sons following close behind. As the chase was underway, William noticed the drops of blood growing, and he soon found the deer's pace slowing. The moment William felt confident, he took the shot, and the deer dropped.

"I am sorry, Father," Seth apologized as they prepared the area to cut up the deer.

William smiled at his son. "It is all right. Most people miss on their first shot. It's only natural."

This seemed to minimize Seth's concern, so he started setting up camp as his father managed the deer, and Samuel went off to retrieve their travois from their last camping site.

They all enjoyed a meal of fresh-cooked deer that night, and after storing the meat away beside the cubes of ice they had brought along in the travois, they settled down for the night. William slept near the pack with his rifle near, with concern of wild animals smelling the fresh meat.

Night passed without any complications, however, and they were soon packed up and on their way home. The day was pleasant, and both the boys were enjoying taking their turns leading the pack horse. They briefly paused to take a drink from a river when the sound of a rifle discharge echoed in the mountains around!

William waited, then attempted the calculations of distance and area before directing his sons to take cover in the brush around. He rushed off toward where the sound came from. He slowed as he neared the area, but as soon as he heard a man moaning from a clearing beyond the forest, he hurried over and found him lying on his back with torn clothes and bloody claw marks across his body.

William attempted to find out what had happened, but the man could only moan and say, "Bear…bear."

Peering around the mountainside, William spotted a cave. He shook his head, picked up the man, and carried him back to where his sons were still hiding.

As soon as he appeared carrying the wounded man, he sons appeared from the brush.

They gave him questioning looks as he set the man down, but did not speak, waiting for instruction to assist.

"Sam, take my hatchet and crush up some ice from one of the cubes. Seth, look around here and find some sage. Bring me a bunch. Quickly now!"

Steadily but quickly, they worked together. William applied the sage to the cuts, and then applied ice chips on top to try to numb the pain. As they waited more for the man's moaning to calm down, William and his oldest son built another travois to carry the man on. The moment it was finished, they placed the man on it and started back for home, both travois in tow.

The trip was difficult, and they had to make brief stops to accommodate the stranger. Before the day was ended, their cabin was seen before them. William cracked a smile and pulled with extra strength. Upon their arrival, the meat travois was taken to the ice by the two boys, and the stranger was carried and placed on William and Jenny's bed.

"Who is he?" she questioned as she set about to give his cuts proper attention.

"Not sure his name. Probably someone who does not know the woods too well," William replied. "But from his torn, fancy clothes, I would say he's from a city somewhere around here."

"Right," she nodded. "They did not do him much good though."

"No, they did not," he agreed.

"If you need to, go take care of the meat," she started, briefly looking up at him. "I think Beth and I have everything under control here."

He looked over their work briefly and then gave a slight nod. "All right. I will send one of the boys back just in case you need them."

Departing, he did as he said he would. Not long after, they had most of the meat hung up in the smokehouse, some in the ice house, and brought a decent size to the kitchen.

The family took turns watching the stranger and caring for him, until he awoke.

As soon as William deemed the man able to be questioned, he began by asking where the man was from and why he was out alone.

Enjoying a bowl of stew, the man began by introducing himself. "My name is Elijah Davis, and I am with the Western Virginia Fur Company of Davis and Davis. There is a large demand for black bear hides at this time, so my group and I were out hunting. Although through some difficult circumstances, I had parted ways with my group several days ago. I decided not to return empty-handed though, and here I am."

"Well," William began, "After you are fully able to travel, I strongly advise you to return to Virginia. People around here don't take too kindly to Easterners coming and killing off the animals just for the fur. You got off easy with scaring the mama black bear instead of being caught poaching by the Indians. You would probably not be breathing right now. I would not say anything to the settlers around here, but they tend to find out things on their own."

Elijah had paused his eating upon hearing all this, and as soon as William finished, he handed back the unfinished bowl of stew. "I understand what you mean. I feel well enough at this moment, so I should probably head out while there is still daylight."

"That would probably be best," William agreed.

Elijah got together his things, and was soon thanking the family and heading out the door.

William handed Elijah his rifle, but reiterated "You remember what I said. Only use this for hunting or self-defense."

"Yes, sir. Only for self-defense. I will let my father and uncle know exactly what you said."

"You do that," William replied, and as Elijah was heading out and waving goodbye, William called out after him, "Make sure to stay away from those mama bear caves. They tend to feel threatened when you get too close to their youngens." He finished with a smile.

"Yes, sir," Elijah waved. "Thank you again."

The family waved one last time, and William picked up Beth.

"Father," little Beth began, "Why does the mother bear feel threatened when Mr. Davis walks close to her babies?"

William smiled and answered, "The mama is afraid of anyone she does not know. She does not want her babies to get hurt."

"Oh, I understand."

As everyone had retreated inside the cabin, young Seth poked at Samuel. "See, I told you there are still bears." Saying this, he jumped on the older in a playful wrestle.

# Fear of the Unseen

*LONE* and traveling in the dark, Elbridge Lawrence slowly walked on the edge of a shadowy forest in an area deserted for miles. Not another soul could be heard, except a cool gloomy breeze, leaves rustling in the trees, and his slow footsteps.

He stopped, realizing he shouldn't go on, not in as thick of darkness as there was. There had been moonlight to travel by, yet as he began walking beside the forest, thick clouds blew across his only light and shadowed the moonlight from him and him from distinguishing his direction.

His first thoughts were to make his own light—a nice warm fire to give what little light it could and offer any little comfort.

Laying his pack in a certain spot under a large willow, he set about collecting tree limbs, small sticks, and as many dry leaves as he could, for there was a slight dew upon the ground, and it made it quite difficult to find such items dry.

At last he had gathered a large quantity, and began preparing a fire, but kept it small to keep it under control.

Soon there were slight flames rising from the wood, and he, sitting on his pack, began to warm himself and feed the fire when necessary.

It was not long before he was somewhat comfortable. In watching the flames, his eyelids began to fall. He began to fight it slightly, just to keep from falling into the fire, when, through an eerie breeze, he heard leaves rustling on the ground–a rustling such as footsteps. Then came a sound such as a low blowing, which sent goosebumps up his arms!

It almost seemed unearthly, yet he edged off his pack and slowly eased an old pistol from it. He turned quietly, trying to make out where the sound was coming from, for he heard it from slightly behind him, deeper into the forest.

He could not see anything, yet before he realized it, the sound was no longer there!

Trying to shrug it off, he excused it by blaming his imagination, for he knew he was one to imagine such wild things.

No sooner had he turned back to the fire, than it began again, yet more quiet, as if distant.

Without a second thought, he grabbed a large limb half protruding from the flames, and, using it as a torch, jumped up and began after the sound, quietly, yet slightly quick.

No sooner had he started off, than he did not hear it. Pausing, he waited until it began again, and it did so several times!

The chasing led him deeper into the forest, until finally, he realized what he was doing and stopped!

Turning, he tried to make out his campfire, but nothing was to be seen! Where could he be? Sickness gripped his stomach, and he began to wildly search around, though not daring to move more than a few feet!

His search was useless, and he had to stop to give moments to thought. Suddenly, he came upon iron spikes piercing up from the ground!

With better search, he found them to be an old rusted spiked fence, enclosing an odd area.

He decided to follow it and walked until he found a gaping hole, which, with some examination, he found to be where a gate had once stood, which now lay tarnished and under dead leaves and twigs.

When he pushed the gate aside, sweeping leaves and twigs along, he found an old, moss-covered, stone path, leading in and out of the enclosed area.

His imagination and curiosity led him in, and he followed the stone path, when, abruptly, the path stopped, in what seemed the center of the area!

As far as he could make out, nothing interesting was in there, yet there was something odd in a mound of the ground, just steps from the path.

Creeping on the mound, he found what he thought might be the beginning of another path, but stepping on it, he almost slipped, for it was not embedded in the ground.

Holding himself, he knelt and brushed away the leaves, revealing the stone in the shape of a headstone!

That was when he realized what kind of mound it was. He gulped a long and dry swallow. With the small glow of his torch, which was by now mostly gone, he could make out worn scratches in the stone, but he didn't care. All he wanted was to be out of there!

Standing, he hurried to find the entrance. Finding the path, he quickly made his way back. Just as he neared the entrance, he stopped dead in his tracks, almost tripping backwards!

There, in front of him, nearly barring the entrance was as deathly a figure as he could imagine!

The form almost appeared human, but was monstrous! Could it be the ghost from that very grave?

The ghost gave a hideous noise, as if speaking, but just stared!

Without thinking, Lawrence raised his flintlock pistol and fired, but the bullet seemed to go through the ghost! Of course, in all the haunted stories that were told Lawrence, no one was ever yet able to destroy a ghost. Letting out a blood curdling cry, he shoved past the ghost and ran for everything he was worth, screaming half the way!

He ran and ran, only slowing seconds to check over his shoulder. When he did, he didn't see anything, though he knew for a fact that a ghost could easily catch up to him!

While running, pictures of monstrous figures flew through his mind. Oh, how could it be? He was told it was only in the stories, yet he knew never to believe them. This was all real!

He almost had thoughts of slowing, when out from in front of a tree he was passing, a deathly hand jumped out, grabbing his face and shoulders, and slinging him backwards! His head hit a hard object and he fell unconscious.

Lawrence's eyes opened. Where was he? What was he doing lying on his back? He could ask himself many other questions, but, first, he must get up.

He tried sitting up. At least he thought he did, but it was as if he was paralyzed! He couldn't move, but he must!

He lay there and struggled. Struggling just to move his fingers, and feeling drops of sweat trickle down his face.

Finally, after what felt like an eternity, he managed to move his fingers, and then the rest of his body began to recuperate.

Sitting up, he tried to inspect his surroundings, and that was when he realized he was mysteriously back at his camp. The fire was just glowing coals, and his pack did not appear touched. Gathering more twigs and small broken tree limbs, he built the fire back up.

Sitting with his back to the fire, as close as he dared, for it was wet from the ground dew, he tried to remember all he could of what had presently taken place.

He sat and thought, and remembered, his back growing warm and dry by the minute. His eyes began to droop again, when again out of the dark came an inhumane cry, such as sounding a cry for help!

Trying with all his might to control himself, he chose a large stick, allowed an end to burn in the fire, and started out again for the ghostly sound.

He again listened and followed, for the cry was repeated and paused, on and on, until he felt he could get no closer to the sound.

The sound appeared to be almost directly underneath his feet, when he stepped out into nothingness!

Grabbing and clawing, he tried for anything that would keep him, and he was able to take hold of an outgrowing tree root before his body flung into empty air!

Swinging wildly, he hit the side of a cliff rather abruptly, which steadied his swinging, but bruised him somewhat.

That's when something, or rather someone, began speaking to him.

"Thank goodness I'm not the only one out here. It's been mighty creepy." He turned to his right to see the form of a young man, holding tight to jutting rocks. "But it turns out, we're in the same predicament," the man observed.

"Well," Lawrence grunted, "Hold on a minute, and I'll get us both out of here."

He was able to pull himself up by the root, and with some difficulty, climbed back on top of the steady cliff ground.

Just as soon as he was steady, he moved over and helped his hanging partner up as well.

The young man thanked him, and brushing off, said, "I'm really glad I found you…I mean, you found me. These woods are haunted."

"You as well, huh?" Lawrence wondered.

"If your meaning being haunted, yes." He began his story of traveling through the woods, and hearing strange things, such as crackling and leaves rustling like someone walking, and of seeing eerie glows. Then he had heard something, or someone, following him. He told how, when he came up on some old, small, fenced area, he saw a ghostly figure come out of a grave, having a glowing fist. The ghost walked his way. He had been paralyzed and could not move any which way, not even when something cracked. Only after the ghost came running after him, was he able to move and run. He had run some distance when he noticed it wasn't following him, so he slowed, yet continued at a walk, and ended up sliding off the edge of the cliff, able to grab on before plunging to his death.

With the story unfolded, Elbridge Lawrence realized what had really all happened, and how he had allowed his imagination run wild.

Leading back to his camp, they both had a good night's sleep. The next morning, they continued their travel together.

# As You Would Them To You

*ARK* gray clouds covered the sky, shadowing the bloody and appalling scene which had happened that day. In addition, a thick fog of smoke floated over the brutal field.

Two opposing armies had met earlier that week. One army's color, a solid dark blue, the other, an iron gray. Flags differed, leaders differed, numbers differed, and causes differed. One the attacker, the other a defender. Who was mighty? Who was strong? Who was the lesser and weak?

Sighting the field, one would not know who the victor was and who was defeated. Hundreds from either side, dead and dying, littered the soil.

Destruction was done–the horror of war. Blood stained the earth and foliage. Many bodies were dismembered, with munitions alike.

Soldiers, crying out in pain, could be heard. Some moaning and asking for just a little water to relieve their dry and parched throats, yet there was no one except the fellow sufferer.

A certain young man lay among the sufferers, he with his own anguish and pain. The torn rags upon his back were of a faded and stained iron gray.

This young soldier, a casualty of war, lay there, unable to move. During the bloody battle with many other wounds, one of his legs was severed from cannon fire, and his other was battered beyond use.

The only fortune he held in that dark and menacing dusk was from a little water in a canteen, yet, not being plentiful, he had only taken small swallows in his most painful moments, and was able to make keep.

Laying there in agony, he was unable to recall any certain moments, yet was held in the present to lay and wait for help, or for death to take him from his suffering.

As he waited, he began to distinguish some cry, nearer, calling for just some relief. Turning his head to search for the fellow sufferer, he found the body not but a few yards away. He thought a moment, and felt sympathy on the man in pain. He began to leave thoughts of his own suffering, and wished to help the other.

Strapping the canteen across his shoulder, he began pulling himself to the fellow victim of the former conflict. The crawling was exceedingly painful, yet his thoughts were not of that, but to help the other.

It was difficult in many ways. His trail made him climb over the dead, and where it was possible, pull himself around the many obstacles. With the loss of blood, before he was able to tend what little he could to his wounds, the loss of strength was as well a hindrance.

Most exhausted as he reached the crying soldier, he paused briefly before speaking, and offered his canteen.

"There is not much, but you are welcome to the rest."

As he was offering, he was able to observe the fellow sufferer.

The man was some years older and much rougher in complexion, yet was gritted much in torment. Blood ran from his brow, soaking what might have once been a white kerchief, yet now crimson. The dying body of the soldier had been pierced with shrapnel and cut by bullets. The color on his back was undistinguishable from the stain of dirt and blood.

Hesitantly, the soldier reached out a soiled, crimson-stained hand, brought the canteen to his lips, and began slowly ingesting the cool, soothing liquid.

After several slow and deliberate swallows, the older man offered the canteen in return.

The younger refused. "I said you may finish it, so it's all yours. Anyway, you seem to need it more than I."

With a rasping voice, the elder spoke, "I don't know how else to thank you, but to just say thanks."

"Your gratitude is accepted. The thought of helping a fellow sufferer is thanks enough to my conscience."

Quietness interceded in what time the older again took a swallow of the cool water, feeling slightly more refreshed as he did.

The older was in some puzzlement, and had to ask, "But why would you, a Rebel, help a dying man as I?"

"First, because I cannot distinguish the color of your once proud uniform, and secondly…"

"I have fought for the Union army," the dying soldier interjected.

"Of which I am sure you fought and suffered well for. Though I am in what was once a proud, distinguished, gray uniform, and am content to fight for the Confederate cause, I also strive to live by a certain most excellent rule."

"And what is that?"

"The most important one."

"What?"

"Do unto others as ye would them to you."

"I still do not understand," he commented, letting his head drop in shame.

"It is rather simple, and can be easily understood. An example is our predicament. We are both wounded and casualties of war. If I could not distinguish colors, it would not matter any to me what color you wore. It only would matter that I should not fight for fear of killing the wrong person. I would not know who was against me. With the God-given compassion, I would be duty-bound to help any wounded and dying soul which should come to me. The colors and sides would not matter, and they should not matter here. We are both dying and should be blind to color."

To this, the elder, though strong and firm, turned his face slightly, trying to hide the moist of his eyes.

"It is all right, and very understandable," the younger admitted, laying in filth, yet joyfully compassionate. He, giving the other time to let his tears run down, began conversation.

"I am of the fifteenth of the army of First Virginia." The elder at this time was returning to face his companion of now. "I come from a small community sixty miles from Richmond. You, sir, where are you from?"

"We were neighbors once then," the older told him. "I am from the twenty-fifth of Maryland."

"Suppose this war would have never happened. We would have probably remained in our own state and never met each other. I would have never had the privilege of befriending and assisting you in your time of need."

"I would have not left my farm in Maryland, nor my family, and never had the time to meet such a kind, gracious man as you. I thank you again."

"It is my pleasure to be of assistance in your time of need. My greater wish, though, is that we will be helped in time. I should not like to see us suffer after such a befriending."

"Neither I. I feel in time the victor will send back the medical wagons if they believe there are yet people to save."

"I suppose we should wait then."

The other agreed, and they waited with little conversation, every moment becoming nearer of friends.

The time did come when wagons were heard, and men were shouting orders for others to search for the living.

The hopes of both men were raised as the voices neared, yet there was a slight fall in the former Confederate soldier's hopes as he found the nearing help to be that of the Federal army, though he continued to look forward to what help could be given him.

The wounded Yankee called out to the group of soldier, as they were near enough.

"Hail to those men fighting for Old Glory!"

Hearing this proud and distinguishable address, two rushed over to him.

"And praise be to any who can aid," he ended when they stood over him.

Quickly, one commanded the other, "Go find an empty stretcher. We need to take this man to the house," meaning one which was nearby, being used for a hospital, as were so many in that area.

The other hurried off and was a while in finding an empty stretcher.

As soon as he returned, they lifted the soldier onto it and began to carry him to the hospital wagon to be transferred.

As they began, he quickly stopped them, "Wait! Do not carry me off until you promise to return for the fellow there in pain as well."

Turning to look, the men realized there was another still breathing and looking after them.

"Let us hurry then," the one commanding said, "We will be back for him as soon as we can."

They left, carrying carefully the elder Yankee in hopes of saving one more comrade. In that time, many well soldiers moved about the field, finding and caring for the live wounded. The smoke slowly lifted, and the haze of war drifted slowly away–for that time at least.

There were many that were helped, but there were many who's souls left this world and passed into eternity.

Those few soldiers did return in hopes to aid that dying man, yet, as they laid aside the stretcher and the one knelt to examine him, he found they were too late. In what time they were not able to be there, he had lost his last blood and had died.

"There can be no help here," the one said. "Let's move on."

For that was only what they could do. Help those in need–those still living.

# The Feeling Within

*THE* reflecting water felt cool against the ankles of Sara as she stood and looked out across the Sea of Galilee. Her day had ended with what she most enjoyed—to walk in the water and listen to the calmness of the waves.

And she did not have to struggle for the calmness of the atmosphere, for she was alone at her small but comfortable place on the beach of that sea. She had never been loved by a man. And so she was never married.

There was a time this beautiful, young, sun looked upon woman loved a certain handsome sir. There was a time when he had noticed her and showed slight feelings toward her. She had thought he loved her at the time.

He had looked at her, smiled at her, touched her hand, and kissed it in bidding good day. In all, his actions created stronger feelings of her toward him.

He would be on her mind almost every moment of every hour of the day. Her longing of him grew to sickness of love for him. Each moment she was able to spend in his presence she tried, in modesty, to show signs of her feelings to him.

However the day came when another fair lady was brought into his life. They were married, and not long after, his command was moved to another area.

His marrying another woman brought her deep anguish. It was as if someone had torn her heart out and every feeling with it.

She lay at nights weeping until there were no more tears to be shed. When her feelings dulled, she decided that was the last she would let herself fall for any man. That was the last she would be hurt.

Instead, she enjoyed the love of nature–for that was something that would never break her. A nice cool breeze set in for the late evening and the time was pleasurable.

At that time, she stood near a lonely chair which sat on the beach, beginning her short walk upon a trail of sand and shells to her quaint house. As she entered the house, she did not feel quite ready to retire, and instead of walking directly to her room, she walked out onto her balcony which overlooked the silent road that led to the British-occupied town of Teir.

This road, which was slightly used in the daylight by British soldiers, cavaliers, and few Jewish peasants, became silent and serene in the evenings and nights.

As she looked out then, she began to hear hoof-beats coming up the road.

Realizing it unseemly for should such riders espy her dressed as she was, she disappeared quickly to the privacy of her chambers and hurriedly clothed in a more covered clothing, returning then with curiosity as to who the late riders would be.

As the soft wind of the outside met her, she found the silent intruders to be a group of three British officers, one in particular she knew of rather well. He was a certain dashing, wise, young leader by the name of Henry Bracklys, a captain whom she recently began to admire and respect.

The men appeared to be worn and tired from a long ride, yet it was another mile to Teir, so she hurriedly sent a young, sleepy, female servant out to beckon them in to tea.

While watching from her large room window, she began to prepare tea and cakes.

As her servant hailed them, she watched as they spoke, and the captain accepted with a kind, grateful word and nod.

With a few glances, she watched them dismount, tie their horses down, and walk toward the house, disappearing from sight as they neared the entrance.

She met them at the door with kind greetings and accepted them gracefully into her tea room. The tea room was the largest of the interior, yet being followed, by little difference, her bed chamber.

In the tea room were large windows, over-looking the peaceful sea, making this room used very frequently by her in times of thought and study. This time it was used to entertain a special guest and his staff.

The tea and cakes were served, and the Captain and miss began conversation.

Being a lady, she was respectfully allowed the first question, and that was of the captain's affairs.

In answer, he spoke with such a determined, yet genial, voice, "We are just returning from army business in Jabesh. I was needed for an inspection of the queen's men there."

"And if I may," Sara continued, "Should your queen take any actions against those recent invaders?"

With a thoughtful sip of tea, the captain answered, "I do not yet know all the details, but I know the soldiers shall be marching to the mountains soon."

"That is good. When my brothers see a strong army behind them, they will fight as well." She was referring to her countrymen.

Silence then fell upon the company as each turned to restful thought and sips of tea.

As the tea drained from the captain's cup, he looked upon his gold watch and found it was time to return on their way.

Waiting a second, he stood and thanked her for so generous of a stay. In his voice was the same tone, yet there was something distinctive. The miss could not quite direct the answer. To her, there seemed something such as some feeling behind his voice. It created something distantly familiar within her, and made something feel as if it fluttered within her.

He bowed benignly, and as they walked to the door, she found it rather difficult to look into his eyes.

As he parted out the door, he turned one last time and looked, with such an enduring look, eternal seconds into her eyes. With a silent, "I will see you again," he departed.

Seeing them out the door, she closed it and leaned against it, somewhat flighty inside, trying then to still herself by laying her hand across her abdomen.

It seemed all familiar, yet why? Why then? Her life seemed all right in those days. She did not want the hurt to return. It was extremely painful. What if it happened again?

# THE PROGRAM

*WE* had been living a normal life. We were happy and content to continue every day. The morning was filled with chatter and a buzz as my siblings and I hurried around finishing our morning chores. It was soon before my brothers and I had to scurry off to our daily study of the Torah and Talmud. I always enjoyed being able to leave the rest of the housework to my sisters, for it was much easier to read and pronounce and listen to the Rabbi than it was to move about the house, scrubbing and patching and whatever else the women of the house do.

My father was the local butcher, and because of that, he could not study as thoroughly as my brothers and I. He did take moments in the evening to read through the Torah, and he was very religious when it came to Rosh Hashanah, Yom Kippur, Chanukah, and, of course, the occasional Sabbath. He was most of all a strong man and a decent provider for the family.

To talk of the family, it was my father and mother, my oldest sister Anka, the next and lightest of us all, Chaya, then there was me, my given name David, and my three younger brothers: Ephraim, Jairo, and Aaron. All were hearty names, at least that is what our father continually told us. Then again, he was never negative when it came to his sons. His continual wish was that we would grow up to become honored citizens of the community and respectful creatures of God.

All this, of course, is to give you some small insight to our family and our lives. It is so that you may sympathize with us as human beings, and not as the beast of the field. Sometimes I wonder if that is what the other kinds of people think of us as, for they dare not bother us or even commune with any of my kind. Our community is a small kernel of corn in a great field. We are like the kernel that is different from the rest. We worship differently, we live differently, and we even sleep differently–that last being more of a guess than a fact.

The only parts of our lives we have in common are that of our language, though it is a second language to us, and that we are all alive, again that last being more of a guess than a fact.

My father says that their worship is considered more of a refined worship. Their Rabbi or Priest wears a big funny hat and speaks in a language that the people cannot understand. My father claims that the only way he knows of these facts was that he was invited to a distant relative's wedding, and the relative was a Gentile. Only in sparing times do our lives connect with the Gentiles, and from what the Rabbi tells us in our study hour, it is a good thing.

The Rabbi explains to us that there is a Gentile, like the Pharaoh of the Torah, who rules this great land, and who the other Gentiles call the Czar. The Rabbi explains that as the Pharaoh of the Torah, we are to respect this Czar and obey his wishes for the time being, but the Rabbi promises that one day, as Moses led the Hebrews out of the land of bondage and sorrow, God will one day lead us out of this land of misery. That is what the Rabbi says.

What is misery? Is misery hard work? That is all that anyone I know has ever known. There are no wealthy people among us. Perhaps some are better off than others, but all work for the food they eat. Even the Rabbi is known to have a small farm to grow to make up for what he does not get as a Rabbi.

The day of lessons was nearing a close, so the Rabbi said our daily prayer and dismissed us, sternly telling us to return at the usual time the following day.

"David?" Jairo questioned. "Do you believe that story about Jonah and that big fish?"

I paused briefly before answering. "Of course. It is in the Torah, isn't it?"

"Yes."

"Then it must be true. God never does or says anything that isn't true."

"Oh, right." Jairo seemed content with my reply.

"David?" This time it was Aaron who questioned. "Do you believe that God is real?"

"Of course I do!" I was bewildered that Aaron could even ask such a question as this.

"But how do you know that he is real if we can't see Him?"

"The same way I know mother made the bread. I do not see her when she makes it, yet I see it when it is made. So I did not see a God when he made us, yet I know that we are alive, right?"

"Oh, right. So there has to be a God to make us people."

"Yes, that is it."

We continued on, it was short distance before we arrived at our dwelling place. It was not a long distance from the school because my father's butcher shop was the front of our house. It was convenient and my father claimed proudly that it saved money.

After changing my clothes, I assisted my father at the butcher shop. He said I was old enough and wise enough to sell and trade, and definitely clean up the tables well. Father said this was a good trade until I found the higher calling, and I was content to follow in my father's footsteps for the time being. I did not see much of a greater future in this town. I did not necessarily want to leave the people I love just to pursue a life of uncertainty. My heart was set on continuing the trade of a butcher, but I left a small opening for becoming a Rabbi. That also might take me away from the people that I loved. Life was definitely not yelling directions to me at that time, and I just did what required doing at the time.

The requirement of that moment was trying to trade a slice of meat to Rivka without her trying to trade my life away to a girl. Rivka is the busybody of our town. She claims to find the right match for a boy and girl, but I have to disagree with her for now, because I would rather live my life without more women in my life. I love my mother and sisters and I dare could not share any of that love with another.

Rivka at this time was talking to me, the other two customers beside her, and my father. She might be the only person that could carry on four conversations in one time as far as I was concerned. I was pretending that I was focused on slicing the meat just right for her, and counting the eggs and placing them where they would not drop and break. Thankfully, once she received the slice of meat from me, she spied another person of importance to talk to, and hurried off to hail them.

My father gave a brief look of relief to me upon her departure and turned to continue his work. I only could smile at his feelings toward her, for they were mutual.

The day went very well. My father and I traded and sold for a good bit of profit. I assisted him in the clean-up while he went over the books and made his corrections and such. Then, we joined the remaining family for our well-cooked evening meal. This meal was perhaps my favorite, for it was the meal in which we all were together as a family. During our morning meal our father was already at work.

The following day was normal, only until I was with my father at his shop.

We were having a particularly slow day. Even Rivka did not come by for her usual slice of meat.

"Why do you suppose there are very few people out today, Father?" I asked as I swatted back a fly.

He turned from his books and looked around. "I truly do not understand. I have not heard if this day has become a religious holiday," he commented partially joking.

At that instant, we heard a loud crashing coming down our side street!

I hurried out of the shop and over to the side street, and was nearly ran over by a rider! Quickly, I jumped back into the shelter of the shop and watched as several other riders flew around the corner. They had clubs, axes, and torches, and were beating, breaking, and torching all the shops, houses, and anything else that might lie around. Fear gripped me inside! What was the meaning of these men? Why were they terrorizing?

My father grabbed the nearest butcher knife and rushed out to try to save the house and the shop. I followed, but carried a branch from the fire. I saw my father lunge at a man on foot. He had barely knocked a window out of our house! The fellow saw my father and the blade he carried, and he turned and ran. As soon as that man left, my father was clubbed by a rider! The club made contact with the back of my father's neck and brought my father to his knees. His knife dropped from his hands.

I rushed over to assist my father in his battle. Swinging my own club as fast and menacing as I could, I finally hit the rider on his thigh and heard him whelp! He took a couple swings at me, but I darted out of harm's way. Seeing he could not hurt me, he turned his horse and rushed off. Quickly I assisted my father inside the house and closed the door behind us.

My brothers and I set a barricade against the door, blocked most of the window areas, and gathered the family in the inner room. With each of us clinging to a weapon of some sort, we waited.

All that time we could hear the screams and crashes! It was terrible! Just as it had started, like the lightning flashes, it ended. There was silence. I gave it a few minutes more before I took away the barricade from the door and peeked out. The ruffians were not there.

I was bewildered. Why would they suddenly appear and then disappear just as quickly?

My father came up beside me, and spoke in such a hush, "It was a program."

# On a Long Journey

*O*H, hunny!" Katherine exclaimed, rushing over to their great, wood barn. "My sister is coming out here to visit!" she finished, waving a telegram in her hand.

Clay Johnson stood from bending over their plow and smiled to his wife. "That's right nice of her."

"I'm so happy," she announced, then accepted his offer for an embrace.

"Does the telegraph tell when she is coming?"

"Oh," she paused briefly. "I was so excited about the news I didn't finish the telegraph." She stood back and continued to read the yellow page. She began mumbling until, finally, she read out loud, "'I will be leaving on tomorrow's train and will arrive around the nineteenth.' My word, that is in four days! I need to hurry and start cleaning!" She turned to head to their home, but stopped long enough to ask, "Do you think you might be able to finish that spare room by then?"

Clay's brow wrinkled. "Well, if I can get Gabe to help me I might be able to, and if the sawmill has the wood I need."

"Could you then?" she asked again with a smile.

"Tell you what, I will check on those if you promise me a delicious meal later this evening," he negotiated with a tease.

She smiled again and returned to her trip to the house.

Clay looked down at the plow, gave a small chuckle, and began hitching up the wagon. He whistled positively to the horses as he hooked them up, and gave each a pat on the neck before he jumped up into the wagon and went on his way to Gabe's place.

Gabe was a single man who had an adjoining stretch of land to the Johnson farm. His could not be called a farm, although he planted a small portion of it. His main source of income and food was hunting. He had plenty of time to gather yarns at the local tavern or general store. Earlier, Clay had talked to Gabe about building an extra room to their house, and Gabe had offered his services. At the time, Clay had turned him down, thinking it could be just a side hobby to work. Now things had changed.

Stopping by the house, Clay found no one home, so he continued on into town and, not to his surprise, he discovered him at the general store.

"Howdy, Clay!" Gabe greeted with a hearty, bearded grin.

"Howdy, Gabe," Clay returned with a smile.

"What brings you to town? Your missus run you out of the house?" he joked, followed by a bellowing laugh.

Clay laughed at Gabe's humor. "No, I am actually just looking for you."

"Me?" he questioned, setting an axe back down in its corner. "What do you need me for?'

"You still able to help me finish that extra room on our house? My wife has family heading this way."

"Hmm, sounds mighty fine. I suppose there would be a small something in it for me," he hinted, giving Clay a searching gaze.

"Keeping your belly full of some of Katherine's good ol' home cooking," Clay replied, knowingly.

"Ha ha. You always could peg my needs. When do we start?"

"Right now, if you can. I need to run over to the sawmill and pick up some more lumber, but then I need to get started on it right after."

"Okay. I'll need to run over to my place to pick up a few things, so I'll meet you out at your's."

"Good. Thanks, Gabe," Clay replied, shaking Gabe's hand and preparing to leave.

"Yes, sir. You just have Kate prepare plenty of vittles, and I'll bring my appetite. Ha ha."

Clay smiled, turned, and walked out the door back to his wagon.

Annette's stomach was jolted as the train went over another one of the many bumps in the tracks. She halfway wished she had refused the sandwich the porter had offered her earlier. Then again, an empty stomach for a full twenty-four hours was not the best idea either, so she quietly endured each jolt as it came.

Excitement raced through her body and grew in anticipation with each mile the train passed. It had been five years since she had last seen Kate and Clay. She remembered when Clay had announced to her and her family that he and his wife were moving out West to claim a homestead. He had seemed so happy, and so had Kate. Although she knew her happiness was doused with quite a bit of stress and worry, Kate had smiled and bravely followed her husband, and they were gone within that month.

Their departure tore at Annette's heart. She and Katherine were very close growing up, and she imagined they would be neighbors when they were both grown and married. Both of these were not true at that time. They were over two thousand miles from each other, and she was not yet married. This last part burdened her the most. She struggled with it immensely ever since her beau had left her the previous year. She was a decent woman according to standards, and could not understand the reasons to her still being single.

This was her main reason for the trip–so that she could put those things behind her and move on. To her, family was what counted the most right now. She could not wait until she was with her sister and brother-in-law, though the last she was kind of hesitant about. She had only known Clay for a short time, and was not for sure if he liked her or not. She knew he loved his wife, her sister, but she was not sure if he loved the rest of the family. She didn't know what she would do if he did not like her as well. It hurt her deeply to think someone might not like her. She had to be on good relations with everyone, and she was determined to find out if he had any problems with her, or if she would have to mend their relationship.

All these thoughts made her even more anxious for this trip to finally come to an end, yet she looked out the window again and watched as nature passed by.

"My, it sure looks like you cleaned out the lumberyard," Gabe joked as he scratched the back of his head and looked at the amount of wood on the back of Clay's wagon.

"You know how it is. Just trying to make sure I have everything I need," Clay replied, jumping off the wagon and walking to the back to unload.

"Well, even if you don't have it all, the lumber yard will definitely have to cut down more trees before they can supply you again," Gabe continued as he began to pull boards out and stack them in a pile.

"You might be right," He agreed, also unloading.

Their work began immediately. Clay had already built the foundation and some of the frame, so they set about completing the frame and beginning a roof. Most of the roof had been completed before the sun went down, so they called it a day and cleaned up for the evening meal.

Katherine had a delicious meal waiting for them when they cleaned up, and they both ate heartily. Conversation was exchanged during the meal with Clay explaining more details to Gabe about the completion of the room.

"I will say this much–it sure is gonna be a large room," Gabe announced.

"Yes, if all goes well, Katherine and I either plan on moving our bedroom into it, or using it for multiple children down the road," he explained. During the last part of the sentence, he reached for Katherine's hand, of which she accepted gently.

Gabe gave another of his famous mischievous, bearded grins. "Got any young'uns in the near future?"

"As far as we know, not yet. You will be among the first to know, don't worry," Clay answered with a grin to his wife.

With the last food off his plate, Gabe joked, "I was just asking, hoping you could have him help you out and let me do my gabbing at Tay's." He was meaning Taylor's General Store.

They all enjoyed his humor, and he then excused himself for the evening. Before he was completely out of house, he stopped. "Oh, Clay, I almost forgot. I had made plans to go out to the Indian village tomorrow to see when they plan on heading out, so if I make it back in time I will only be able to help in the late evening with your room."

"That's fine, Gabe, I'll finish up the roof and we can cut out the doorway if you make it back in time."

"All right. Thank your missus for the delicious meal again for me."

"I will."

Clay closed the door behind Gabe and went to help his wife clean the dishes. Before beginning though, he embraced his wife from behind and she softly giggled.

"A couple of children running around this house would be nice," he hinted with a playful nuzzle to her ear.

"Hunny," she reprimanded. "Can't you see I am cleaning?"

Giving her a quick squeeze before letting go, he responded, "Yes, I do," and stepping beside her, he then began to assist her. "Oh, and Gabe told me to thank you again for the meal."

"I guess with him helping you out with the room I should go into town to get a few more things for meals."

"Right. Although he told me he will not be able to be here tomorrow. He has errands to run."

"Oh. So will you be building any on the room then?"

"Oh, yes, I am not totally helpless without him," he smiled.

"That is not what I meant."

"I know," he replied, after which he planted a quick kiss on her cheek.

They were finished cleaning at that time, so prepared for the night. As they were lying near in bed, Katherine spoke with a soft smile. "You know, one pleasant reason of not having children at this time is that it allows us alone time like this."

He turned to her, "You are right," he said, after which began to give her passionate kisses.

The train came to a jolting halt and startled Annette awake. She had dosed off again, no matter how hard she attempted to stay awake for the day. Only this time, outside the window was dark. At that time, she began to hear the porter call the name of the town they were stopped at as he walked down the cars. It, of course, was not her stop, but she always jumped at the chance to step outside and stretch her legs.

"Mr. Jeremiah!" she called to the porter as he neared her.

"Yes, ma'am?" he questioned.

"How long will we be at this stop?" she asked, already standing up from her seat.

"Oh, no more than fifteen minutes, ma'am. Unless there is a minor delay, of course," he answered with his natural smile.

"Will you step out and make sure I get back in when you are ready to leave? I do not have the time."

"Of course, ma'am, but please do not wander too far from the platform."

"I won't." Saying this, she scooted passed him to the nearest door.

A cool breeze greeted her as she stepped out onto the platform. She gratefully welcomed it as she straightened out her dress. She was not too keen on traveling for days in an enclosed area. Day by day the space seemed to shrink, but she knew this was only her imagination.

Allowing the cool breeze to embrace her, she then decided to take a look around. This town was a quaint town. It was a decent size, but just below the size of being called a city. Besides the few people who had joined her from the train on the platform, there were only few people from the town. One was a police officer, who nodded at her as he passed her on his patrol, another being the station master, and a couple other men who were there to assist in any of the train's needs. At that moment, the conductor called for everyone to come aboard, and seeing the porter wave to her from a door, she stepped back in, and her journey down the endless track continued.

Clay's work was slower that day. Katherine assisted where she could, but that was limited. There was more work that was needed to be done on the roof to keep away the rain, and Clay set about trying to complete this. Climbing around on the frame was delicate, and he began this with precaution.

He was happy as the morning passed and Katherine called up to him that his noon meal was prepared. As they ate on a stack of boards, Katherine talked, and as Clay listened, he went over the partially-completed structure. He was rather disappointed in his slow progress that morning, so he decided he needed to attempt to speed the work up. Upon finishing his meal, he thanked his wife with a kiss to her cheek, and tied up the needed boards to continue the roof.

His pack was heavy and quite awkward to carry up the ladder, but without the extra person, there was no other way to complete the task. When he arrived at the top, he began to tie the rope to part of the frame as he had done a few times that morning, though he was not able to do it completely because some of the boards in the pack got stuck under part of the frame. Grunting to himself, he ventured out on the frame to try to get the boards unstuck. A moment passed before he realized that his position was not the smartest, but before the thought completely passed through his mind, he lost his footing.

He grabbed for the frame frantically! All his hands grasped were the bundle of boards. Falling to the ground, he brought the boards straight down on his arm! The wind was knocked from him as he fell on his back, and a sharp pain shot through his arm and into his body.

Katherine heard the commotion from the barn, and rushed out to find him on the ground, right before she heard him shout in pain.

She ran to him. "Clay! What happened?! Are you okay?! Clay!"

He gave her a brief moment to ask all those questions before called for her to stop. "I can't move my arm, so you will have to help me get these boards off of it. Now, when I say, you lift the boards as much as you can and I will try to pull my arm out!"

"Okay," she choked out in tears. Grabbing hold of the bundle, she waited for his signal, and then lifted. With some strain, she managed to lift them enough for him to pull his arm out.

She was able to help get him inside, laid him down on their bed, and rushed off to get the doctor. The time seemed slowed between the time she departed and the time she returned with the doctor.

The doctor gave him a full examination, and though his process to analysis was limited, he announced, "We definitely know you have a broken arm. Now the bone still seems to be in place, so we will just have to splint it and let the bone heal back. I also believe you have internal bruising. I do not think anything his punctured, but we will have to keep an eye on things just the same. You will need to stay in bed for a few days at least, until we can make sure there is no further damage."

Before the doctor left, he instructed Katherine to restrict Clay's diet to soup until his bruised body could heal.

Katherine returned to Clay's side and sat down, taking his good hand in hers. "Do you need anything right now?"

"A new arm," he partially joked.

She only hinted a smile.

"I'm sorry," he apologized.

"It wasn't your fault. It was just an accident."

"But now we won't have that extra room for Annette."

"That's okay. I am sure she won't mind. There's some sleeping space still in the lean, too. I can just tidy up there for her. In fact, if there's nothing else you need, I'll go do that right now before I finish the chores. "

"Yes, I am fine for now. Thank you."

She leaned down and gave him a kiss. "Now, you get well so we can enjoy her stay together."

"I actually think I like the idea of being laid up in here away from the commotion when it comes," he teased.

She smiled at his humor and gave him a light pat on his good arm. Squeezing his hand gently, she went out to finish her work.

There seemed no end to Annette's journey. She sighed heavily as the train once more stopped for needed fuel. Questioning Jeremiah as to their stay, he assured her it would be several minutes as their usual fuel stops were, so she decided to venture into the town. This was a town with all the hustle and bustle of a busy day that the railroad brought. Though it was not quite as big as the city she was used to, the noise from the saloons and shops around the train station definitely made up for the size.

All the hustle and bustle did not curb her want to discover, however, and she immediately headed to the nearest shop. It was a clothing store, and she was amazed by the attractive dresses that were upon display in the windows. Immediately on entering, she found that the high quality continued into the store. She was delighted to see a city-like shop in the wilderness, but wondered how anyone could wear any of the fancy fabric in this shop, or even afford it for that matter.

An older plump lady looked up from a ledger at the front desk and offered, "May I help you?"

"Oh, I am just admiring. Thank you," Annette replied, letting go of her feel of a sleeve.

"Okay. Please don't soil."

Annette's eyebrow rose. "I will not. I am a passenger from Boston, and I do believe I know how to admire without soiling."

"Oh, I beg your pardon. Let me know if you need my assistance."

"I do have one question."

"Yes?" the lady offered, pulling down her glasses.

"Do you have many customers?"

The lady stood up from her seat before she answered. "Yes, miss, mostly when the trains bring in city folk like you."

Annette muffled a giggle. "Well, thank you for your time. I best be returning to the train."

She took her leave of the shop, and was walking out the door when she was ran into by a young boy.

"Sorry, miss," the boy shouted and hurried off.

She shook her head slightly and brushed off her dress. Before returning to the train, however, she found a vendor and purchased an apple. She was happy to be able to enjoy fresh fruit, for on the train that was one luxury that was lacking.

Slowly she returned to the train, and even more slowly she took her seat. Waiting, she decided to find out the time, and reached for the pocket watch that she kept in her blouse pocket. Her fingers reached down, but only touched the bottom of the pocket! Where could it have gone? Frantically she looked around her seat. Her mind raced to the last moment she knew she had it. She had checked the time briefly before exiting the train, and had made sure to place it back into the pocket, but it was not there now!

She called for the porter and explained to him her dilemma. Their time at that station was very limited, but he promised to look around the exit she took off the train. Continuing her search, she even took to the floor around her seat, but the search was fruitless.

It was not long before the train whistle went off and they jolted in their continued journey. The porter returned to Annette and announced he had not found anything. She thanked him and turned to look out the window, watching the town pass by.

That watch was special to her in a way. It was the only item she had kept from her former lover. She had never returned it, and he had never asked for it, so she kept it. Now it was gone.

Clay was startled awake as he heard a knock at the door, and then a bellowing "Hello?"

"I am in here, Gabe!" he called back.

Briefly, Gabe turned the corner, and gave Clay and questioning look. "What happened to you, Clay?"

"Well, it is rather a quick story actually," he responded as he shuffled slightly in bed. "Yesterday, I was working on the roof. I carried too heavy of a load, and I fell off the roof."

"Oh, dear. Are you going to be all right?'

"The doctor says I will mend, but I cannot do any work for some time."

"I feel awful.  I decide to go on some trip and you end up hurt."

"It's not your fault. It was my own. I should not have been careless."

"Where is your wife's sister going to stay now?"

"My wife has cleaned up the lean-to. She can sleep there."

"But that is a distance from this house. It's not right." Gabe's words trailed off as he began to ponder the issue. "I tell you what. I have a few men in town who still owe me. Let me see what I can do." Without allowing Clay to reply, he departed.

Clay knew what Gabe was conspiring, but he was somehow okay with it, so he closed his eyes and attempted again at his rest. It was not long before he fell into a deep sleep, and did not wake up until the day had passed and his wife had bedded down with him. He smiled to see her beside him, and closed his eyes once again.

Gabe and his group worked on the extension from sunup to sunset, and managed to complete it, furniture and all, the day Annette arrived in a stagecoach. He offered to drive Clay and Katherine into town to meet her, and they gladly accepted.

The stage was late as usual and all the while Katherine attempted with fail to contain her excitement. Clay laughed with his wife, and Gabe stood back to watch the soon-to-be reunion.

Finally the stage arrived, and two people stepped out and were followed by Annette, who immediately embraced Katherine. Tears of joy fell as they exchanged hugs and hearty handshakes.

As the ladies went to climb in the buckboard, Clay stood back to give Gabe a handshake. "Thank you again for all you did for me. I don't know how I could ever repay you."

Rubbing his bear thoughtfully and looking after the ladies, Gabe replied, "There might one way we can call it even…"

"Anything."

"If you invite me to dinner now and then while she is here, we can call it even," he said with a smile.

Clay looked after the ladies, and then looked to Gabe with a smile. "That sounds like a deal. How does tomorrow for dinner sound?"

Gabe took Clay's hand in his, and gave it another good shake. "You got yourself a guest then."

Clay joined his wife and her sister in the buckboard, and they headed back to the farm.

# THE MYTHICAL OR GENUINE RELIC

"I knight thee Sir Francisco Diego. Go now, and bring glory to this kingdom," King Phillip II proclaimed, resting the sword then on the ground.

Sir Diego stood, saluted his king, and turned to leave the court, his circle of followers on his heels.

Diego and his followers were commissioned a ship on which they hurriedly began to prepare for the upcoming mission.

This mission was that of a dangerous one. They were to embark upon a journey to the New Word in search of the tale of a holy relic. It was said that, many years ago when the worlds were connected, ancient tribes worshipped this relic, and it followed them to their latest sighting in the New World. This was a great stone of solid gold, inlaid with precious jewels, on which the words were inscribed, "TO THE GREATNESS OF HEAVEN", in an ancient language.

From the first discovery of this New World by Christopher Columbus, which was clearly accidental, to the few travels of previous explorers, all wanted to be the one bestowed the honor from discovering this great relic. Many of these found gold and great wealth, but none discovered this true relic. The myth continued to announce that the authenticity would be realized, and any replicas would be mischief to their creators.

Many believe this relic was first in the Garden of Eden. Others believe it was created for King Solomon's great temple. Some did not even care of its origin, but all in search of it either wished to benefit in wealth, honor, or both.

The ship was prepared, and the group set sail. There was no grin on Diego's face, yet great anticipation was boiling in his stomach.

Their journey for the next few months was trying and dangerous, yet the majority of the ship's crew and passengers survived the struggles of the water.

Their whereabouts were not exactly known, yet it was roughly estimated they were in the Southern Americas. That is where they wished to be. The smaller boats were dropped to the side of the ship, and the select group set for shore. They did not begin their ventures immediately; instead, they set up camp and a perimeter for fear of the inhabitants of that land. The stories were of monster creatures and demon people. Diego had half a mind not to believe the stories, yet his other half believed anything, so he would not take the chance.

Their first night in that unknown world passed quietly. To Diego, this made him feel even more uneasy, because, to him, it was the unseen that disturbed him the most.

At break of dawn, after a brief morning meal, Diego and his chosen men set out inland in search of their relic. He first contemplated leaving a few men at their beach camp, yet this idea was discarded when he could not obtain any volunteers for this. Instead, he decided it was best for his assembly to stay together in case of adversity.

After following the beach for a distance, they immediately encountered a thick jungle. Four conquistadors were stationed ahead of the group to break a path for the remaining company, two were stationed in the rear to mark the path in case a quick retreat was called for, and one was commissioned in marking down landmarks to create a map of their own.

They followed a rough map designed by previous discoverers, and it was almost useless in the deep jungle, but they continued forward.

Their march was slowed by having to break a path and from the constant catching of brush with their weapons and armor, so it was nearing the night before they were far in their search.

Camp was called, a perimeter was set, large fires were built, and Sir Diego began to number his men. This was done in vigilance of possibly losing any on their day's journey.

After he was satisfied with the number of his company, he bedded down for the night with two guards posted at the entrance of his tent.

As the sun glowed on his tent, he awoke. Before exiting his tent, he took another look at the documents he was sent with: the first was the oldest, a story of the holy relic that was the object of their search, the second was their commission from the mighty King Phillip II, and the rest were rough maps of the New World and tally book of the cost of this expedition. If he were to find this relic, it would be given to the King Phillip's royal collection. The worst case, was, if he were not able to find this relic, his expedition was to be repaid also to King Phillip II.

A time was as well stamped on their journey, and if they did not return within the time given, they would be declared as criminals and a bounty placed on their heads. The thought of whether this trip should have even been tried quickly or not passed through Sir Diego's mind, yet he brushed it off, synched up his sword, and exited the tent.

He directed a head count as the company broke down their camp, and to his greatest fears, he found one conquistador to be missing! Hurriedly, he directed another head count and found it to be true. The camp was forgotten at that moment, and a search was made for their missing man.

It was not long before the conquistador was found a small distance in the brush. He was dead. From his appearance, he had stepped outside the camp perimeters alone to relieve himself, and some venomous animal had found him and bitten him. His cries were not heard because of the thick jungle brush, and he must have laid alone for the time it took him to pass from this world.

His body was taken care of, wrapped, and set on one of their wheeled carts, to be later buried at the edge of the jungle near the beach and their original camping site. Warnings were sent throughout the company once again and they resumed their search.

Sir Diego's mind journeyed through his previous life as the jungle scenery passed by in their march. It was not the most comfortable, yet the fear of death was not sinister as it was at this moment in his life. He remembered his life as a conquistador in the barracks of Spain. He was trained for this moment: through hand to hand combat and from being repeatedly told that he would face danger, but nothing was placed in his mind that felt like the fear that was in it at this time.

A rest was called at midday and the company enjoyed a moment to refresh themselves with needed fresh water and discovered edible fruit from the jungle.

Sir Diego enjoyed his refreshment separated from his company, and observed them as they spoke among themselves in groups. Some spoke low in cautioned voices. One could only imagine what they had in secrecy. Others of the groups spoke loudly with hearty laughs. It was their attempt to make light of their situation, by making tall stories of their past lives. There were a few in the company that sat alone and spoke to no one.

At the proper time, the company was assembled, and they set out once again in like formation as every previous time. At this time, Sir Diego decided to march near his front line of conquistadors, instead of in the midsection as other times.

They had barely set out when, all of a sudden, they heard screams and cries coming from where the bush-whackers were required to be!

Sir Diego yelled for the men to assume defense position and they waited.

They soon heard one of the whackers running toward them and yelling that another was being attacked by a great animal!

Bowmen were summoned, and that group followed the whacker to the area of the attack. They arrived too late! What lay before them was an undistinguishable mess. Wrapping a body was out of the question, but they collected his body armor and weapon and placed it with the body on the cart.

Word started circulating that their journey was cursed, and some even mentioned returning to the ship and Spain, but Sir Diego pushed the conquistadors forward. He was not ready to give up their search over two careless men.

Their day's search ended fruitlessly, but he was sure they were a day closer to finding the abandoned temple where their relic lay. He called to set up camp, and before he bedded down, he gave strict instructions for his men not to leave the perimeter.

He felt as if he had barely closed his eyes when he heard shouts from one of their guards. Hurriedly, he put his armor back and on, and with his sword in hand, he exited the tent.

The camp was in a bustle with men arming themselves and others rushing to a certain area. There seemed not be a noticeable attack, so he called for order, and began to investigate the reason for the guard's calls.

It did not take long for him to find out the issue, because the sight was very obvious. Two guards were tied together with vines, and their heads were slumped over dead! He questioned the guards as to why no one had heard an attack, but all they could show him was a thin needle in one of the dead men's neck, and a crude knife stab in the other guard's back.

He directed for every man to light a torch and for the fires to be stirred. That night, everyone remained awake for fear they would be next.

The next day, camp was struck, and they continued their search. All eyes were heavy for lack of sleep, but no one dared let their guard down for fear of death. Sir Diego noticed every man would jump at the slightest sound that they heard.

Their days continued without them finding the relic they searched for. Many of them became down-hearted, and a group attempted to retreat to the ships, but their bodies were found mutilated and bare. In the remaining group, some had jungle fever, and others were weak with exhaustion. Sir Diego knew in his heart they would most likely never find their relic, but he did not have any means of repaying King Phillip II's coffers, so he continued and decided he would find the relic even if he had to cross from sea to sea.

One day as they rested (for their rests were more frequent in those later days), they began to hear strange noises coming from the brush around them. No sooner did the noises begin that arrows and spears came flying towards them!

Sir Diego attempted to call his men to arms, but it was almost useless as one man after another fell, struck by the missiles!

Painted human savages followed the volley of missiles. They all brandished knives, spears, and clubs of all sorts.

In the following year, King Phillip II put out a warrant for Sir Francisco's and his company's arrest, but they were never found, and many still wonder of their locality.

Some speculation is made in the town taverns that the company found the relic and decided to steal it, and they now live as rich esquires in lands far away. Others attempt to defend them and claim the group met with misfortunes, but no one has attempted to search for the lost relic ever again. One must wonder if it even exists…

# A Price Paid
# At Concord

*A*S the battle was finished, the men were set about the task of burying the dead and caring for the wounded. There were few doctors in the larger militia, totaling one hundred thirty-four, and several were in need of medical treatment.

The sight of death was familiar to Ashworth, yet his son, the innocent, had not viewed death. As he and son had the task of burial, the sight was most unbearable to the younger man. He became wrenched within his abdomen. As the sickness engulfed him, he began to feel light and swayed slightly, leaning upon the shovel to steady, though trying to conceal his sickness.

His father, aware of most of his son's movements, observed his sway and motion to steady his head, though instead of speaking directly, he began, "The sight of death is most unbearable, particularly to the innocent. Even I have trouble keeping my insides stable."

An elderly sir, by slight years, spoke to this remark, "Indeed, I have been in wars past, yet the sight is always difficult to view. I shall not feel the same for days."

"I have never killed a person until this day," Henry acknowledged vocally.

"I can remember that day I was called upon to kill fellow beings," his father recalled. "It was not celebrated. It was sorrowed and mourned. It is something not to be considered. It must be passed as a duty to family and country. We must keep the mindset. If we were not to do this, our families may be the ones to die, and that is more unbearable to think upon to me, as I believe it is to all others likewise."

To this, Henry nodded and the other agreed, "Indeed."

The dead were buried, and the militia returned to their encampment to train and wait for additional orders. That evening as the men settled for the day's end, there were many things to ponder.

John Ashworth sat on his makeshift bed, holding the dear reminder of his little young flower. It was almost as a tear drop was restrained in his eye. He was never one to weep openly. Only a minor amount of choice times was he noticed to weep, but he was not to weep then. His heart was heavy, as a father leaving his dear beloved children.

Since the day his significant other passed from this mortal earth to an immortal being, he had grown to love and care for his young in a nearer respect.

Not once had he ever lessened in love to his children, yet it was something else–a closeness to remain to care for them as he had always, yet to begin to endeavor caring for them as she had in some sense; to watch their every step, keeping from harm or injury. However, when harm or injury was felt, their mother was not there for pity of pain. It was him they desired to lessen their pain and hurt. His task as a parent had become more difficult, yet it had brought him nearer to understanding just what they felt, and he truly missed them at this time.

Ashworth lay down and fell into a light slumber with them upon his mind. It was difficult to obtain even a fitful rest with worries upon his mind, and he sat awake at the hour before sunrise. At the strike of morning, each man was called upon to assume ranks for an important task.

The colonel ordered a quick march into Massachusetts to a certain city called Concord, where it was heard a large quantity of Colonial arms and munitions were being held, and under extreme risk of being captured. The camp was struck, and with each Patriot carrying his load, they set out.

In this march, there were no pleasant animal creatures scurrying about in entertainment. There was no lovely song of the bird. This was war, and all of God's earthly creatures knew the meaning of war. Lives were taken and blood was shed. The drops of crimson spilt for dear ones and for country, the dearly beloved, and the stranger never seen or heard of before. It was a just cause and everyone within themselves knew it.

Marching was toilsome, yet in the count of defending helpless lives, it was not to be counted. Of the men, many marched with kindred: a son, a brother, or a father. Many marched and before this war was to end, many would perish.

As the days led on, many more Patriots joined their small band, increasing it as they proceeded on. Within days of crossing the colony border line of Massachusetts, scouts informed them that the munitions at Concord had already been captured and burned by a certain English Colonel, Francis Smith, under the orders of General Thomas Gage. However, they were to continue on to join Colonel Barret of the colonial regulars.

Having thus proceeded after obtaining the necessary force, it was a race between the loyal yet lesser Patriot force and the much larger British force, who was ready to slaughter any who should stand in defiance.

I should ask, where should be evil stopped, if all defiance flees? When evil is assured of victory, they shall proceed for more. They will not end until every portion of earth is theirs. That is why we should stand and end any of evil and its attacks.

A forced march was needed of the Colonists and in days they joined the small force of Colonel Barret. Thanks be to the Heavenly Being above for fellow persons who should stand in line with you and assist in the struggle against evil.

As the two forces united, morale was brought to the older, who had fought some, yet felt insignificant. Together they set about building blockades on the edge of the town, opposite the Concord River. Their defense was of bagged sand, upturned wagons, and loose large objects made in to defense walls.

To be most prepared for the oncoming red-cloaked army, scouts were sent ahead to espy their position. They were watched and reports were made of their distance at intervals of half an hour.

Quickly and dexterously, a defense was built, and there was time for the Colonist army to await the coming of the enemy. At last, the word was brought in from the scouts that the enemy was near and would be marching on them in moments. Even with the scouts joining the armed Patriots, the defense army numbered not as many as the army marching then toward them and the town of Concord.

The leading officers, Colonel Wester of the Connecticut volunteers and Colonel Barret of the Massachusetts regulars, watched the enemy near at a distance from a single field telescope.

The command was given to prepare–to prepare one's self with God and man, lest he should pass from this mortal earth and awake at that Day of Judgment. And of you, perhaps not fighting a battle or preparing to kill or be wounded it is of greatest importance you should ready yourself.

The day may come when least expected that you fall and enter the immortal world. There are places beyond our grasp of thought where immortal beings dwell. Take heed to the words of wisdom from those everlasting Holy Scriptures.

The day was yet at its beginning as the militia awaited. Even as the sun shone, a cool late winter breeze brushed across the chilled men. No one knew where it had come from. The month was April, and winter had long passed. Perhaps it was something sacred dedicating those who were to pass away. Who was to know?

Like the last battle, there was a time of patience, a time for thoughts. Yet the knowledgeable men did not put such thoughts of the soon-to-come battle into their mind. There were a few who did think upon the battle, and fear seized the weak among them. Their courage began exhausting, and it was all they could muster to hold.

The moment the red line became visible, it became extremely difficult for those feeble. As it slowly neared, drops of perspiration soaked their brows, wetting wherever it dropped.

At last, the time was too tense for such as they, and suddenly, one leaped up from his kneel behind the defense wall, threw his fire weapon to the ground, and retreated at a run. With this bold insubordination, three more followed in fear.

In these actions is courage not shown–to desert the companion soldier in time of battle. To discourage any additional deserting, the Colonel had the officer and choice trusted men stand behind the soldiers, and he yelled, "Any next deserting shall have a fate worthy of his courage! Now look ahead, the enemy is before, not behind!"

At this time, the enemy was before, yet slightly without range of musket shot. The red line stopped at this distance, and officers began to evaluate the conditions. With a moment to consider, a mounted officer was chosen among them, and, bearing a white cloth upon his drawn saber, he proceeded half the distance to the awaiting militia.

It was chosen, since Colonel Barret was of the Massachusetts colony, he was to meet the British officer, and he went merely on foot to meet a mounted courier. Leaving his musket and taking only his small arm, he walked until he was opposite the other.

"I am emiss'ry of Colonel Smith's royal British army and I 'ave come here with terms."

"I shall listen to what is proposed."

"The impartial wishes of Colonel Smith and his army are for your militia to surrender your body and lay down your weapons. He then will allow you to return to your homes."

To this, the Colonel acknowledged with an undaunted nod. "Very well. Now hear our terms."

The English emissary chuckled in disparage, "I do not believe you are in po'sition to give terms."

"Given that we are in possession of weapons able to fire and hold a defense, we are equal for terms of our own to be heard."

"Very well. Continue," he responded, though spoken impassively.

"First, I would have you know there are militias of us from other Colonies, and there are more of us than are seen.

"On our terms, you may tell your English colonel to command his troops to lay down every weapon that was brought here to be used against us and return in full parade to England—"

"The colonel—" the emissary interrupted.

"I have not yet ended!" Colonel Barret commanded. With his silence, he continued. "In your return, stop at every Colonist home and beg forgiveness for every deed the King and Parliament has committed against us, swearing there to never take up arms against the colonies again! That is our proposition, and you may deliver it to your commanding officer."

Without further words, the colonel turned about and returned to the defense, knowledgeable of what the reply should be. He watched, through the telescope, the messenger return and converse with, what was assumed, the commanding officer.

Then, as an answer, the messenger threw down the white flag, trampled on it in full view of the militia, returning then to ranks.

"The answer is war!" the colonel shouted for all to hear.

The red line immediately returned to march onward to them.

"Do not fire until they are well within range and there is no retreat for them!" was the command from the officers. To which the men waited and prepared, anxious for what the coming battle might bring. At that time, Ashworth spoke a word of encouragement to his son. "Do not lose spirit, my son. As the Lord gave us the battle before, he shall so surely give of this."

With fear, yet calm eyes, the young lad turned to his father, and said, "Can you be sure, Father, that the whole of us will come through this battle victorious?"

These words struck the father's heart. He could not be sure. He wanted to be, yet in war, some men are destined to die. To his son's question, he answered, "The Lord shall give us this day. Do not lose hope!"

His son returned to watch the nearing bright, paraded regiment, which was now steadily nearing within an eighty yard range.

As the sun was seen moving, the English regiment neared within the seventy…and the sixty…the fifty-five…and the forty, at where they stopped. As they began positioning to fire, the command was given for the militia to fire upon them!

Again the sound of battle could be heard as the musketry split the silence. The sight was so atrocious once again.  Musket balls pierced the bodies of the regular army. Blood spewed of many persons. Many of the regiment fell to the earth. Their last deeds were done.

Many officers were killed in the first slaughter, yet many were there to keep the command and the army held. In war there are terrible sights, appalling, and not fit for the society of man. However, man is the maker of war, and with the beginning of war, there is not an ending until the world is at end.

Fire was exchanged on either side, the British regiment in more orderly fashion and the defenders after every loading. At a moment, a musket ball passed very near the ear of Ashworth, and he heard it embed in a stationary object behind him. Searching to see just where the shot might have come from, he found an officer leveling his carbine and preparing to shoot once more upon Ashworth!

Hastily, Ashworth aimed and discharged his musket! The ball pierced the mid-center neck of the officer. For a second, the officer stood stunned, yet dropped his firearm and he then dropped to the cold earth. Lifeless blood began pouring from his wound.

Hurriedly, the victor loaded and fired again at other soldiers wearing red, tyrannical apparel. The day slowly began to favor the Colonist militia–slowly the British line fell, slowly victory was seen. John turned to speak a quick word to his son.

However, those words never left the lips of the father. As he turned his eyes upon his son, a musket ball pierced the abdomen of his son! The young man gasped in pain and fell back.

Forgetting all else, John Ashworth left his musket, and rushed to kneel at his son's side. He looked into Henry's eyes. Death was coming upon him. A slight spittle of blood crept down the side of his mouth. Searching the wound, he found it to be fatal. The time of his son remaining with him upon that earth was nearing an end.

Lifting the head of his boy into his lap, he looked into his dying Henry's eyes. As the impact shock subsided, Henry managed to look up with a cloudy gaze into his father's eyes. Slowly, he began to struggle to move his lips, and spoke almost in a whisper, yet with a slight smile upon his face.

"Please carry on this war, for liberty of what I now can feel. Carry on, I do implore, do not let it be silenced or kill..." Henry's lips quivered to continue, yet he could not. With a last gaze into the eyes of his father, he passed from this mortal earth into immortality.

## Dear reader,

Though this book may be filled with choice poems and stories, it does not amount to much if it does not give the Gospel also.

There is nothing mentioned in these stories of how a person may receive salvation, so now I would like to give you those simple steps.

First Romans 3:23 says "For all have sinned, and come short of the glory of God;"

We have all sinned. I have sinned, and you need to admit that you have sinned, too. And, since we have sinned, what does that make us? A sinner, plain and simple. Because we have sinned, we come short of God's glory.

Also, Romans 3:10 reads, "As it is written, There is none righteous, no, not one:"

Here it plainly restates, **We have all sinned.**

Now Romans 6:23 says, "For the wages of sin is death:"

Let's pause right here. What does this tell us? It doesn't just mean we will die physically, though everyone dies sooner or later. Dying is a part of living. But this verse tells us that after physical death, there comes a spiritual death. The spiritual death is when a person goes to Hell, where there is **eternal** pain, torment, and suffering. But let's continue with the verse.

It reads, "…but the gift of God is eternal life through Jesus Christ our Lord."

A gift is something someone gives you, without any charge, right? For instance, a person wouldn't give you a brand new car as a gift, and then tell you that you owe them the amount the car is worth. No, a gift is free! That means God is giving you the **gift** of eternal life, which is salvation, through Jesus Christ.

*And what does "through Jesus Christ" mean? When Jesus came down from heaven, he lived a perfectly sinless life. Then he went through extremely painful torture, when he died to pay for our sin. The Bible even says that he wasn't recognizable as a human being, when he died on the cross. This verse says "the wages of sin is death," that means we all would be going to Hell if Jesus hadn't died on the cross. But he didn't just die and stop there. No, he rose on the third day. By doing this, he made it possible for* **all people to be saved.**

*Because he did all that for us, all a person has to do to receive this* **free gift**, *is ask Him into their heart. Just pray a prayer, it doesn't matter how long, or how short it is, just sincerely pray and ask Him to forgive you, acknowledging him as your Savior, and receive His free gift.*

*And please do not wait, do it now!*

*Sincerely:*

*J. A. Irvin*